This book belongs to

....

Written by Sarah Creese.
Illustrated by Lara Ede.

sparkle town fairies

Alice
the
Amber
Fairy

and the Showstopper Spectacular

Sarah Creese ✷ Lara Ede

make
believe
ideas

In **Sparkle Town**, for all to see,
there stood a dazzling store
full of **amber instruments**,
and with a **singing** door!

Main Street

Chief Creator of things to play,
for every kind of sound,

was **Alice** the **Amber Fairy** —
the best inventor around!

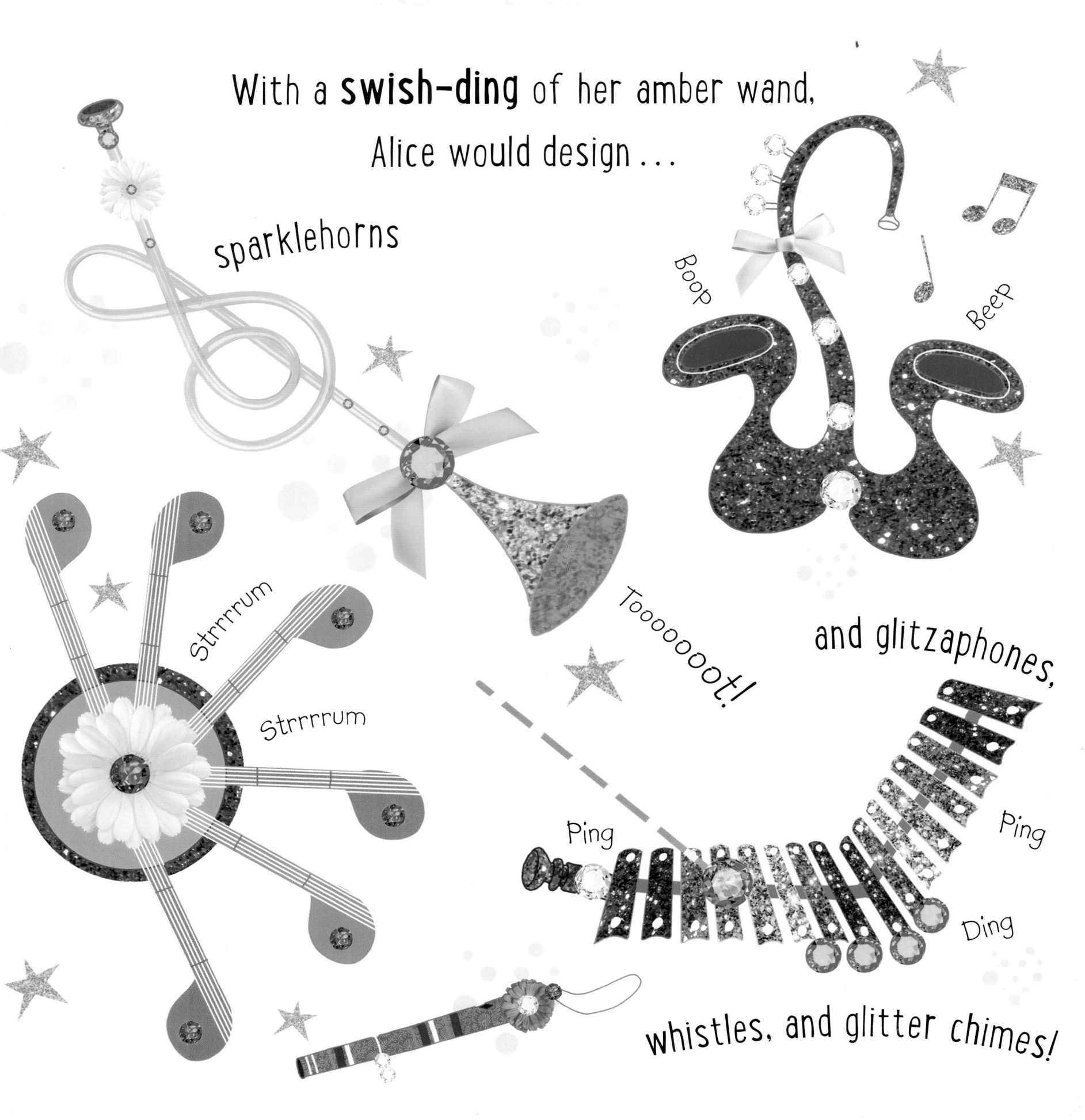

Every **ten years** in Fairy Land,
a contest came to town
to choose a **fairy winner** for
the SHOWSTOPPER SPECTACULAR crown.

Main Street

It's Showstopper time!

Yours sincerely

Juno Jewel

SHOWSTOPPER SPECTACULAR Head Judge

·

All tuneful entries will be welcomed,
but only one will be worthy of winning the crown.

·

Fairy Land's greatest musical contest!

SHOWSTOPPER SPECTACULAR

We proudly present the

Dear Fairies,

The **Amber family** fairies had won year in, year out.

Alyssa Amber

Alfie Amber

1st

Annie Amber

Alex Amber

Astra Amber

Amelia Amber

Amy Amber

The Ambers are musical masters!

So Alice's friends thought she would win —
of this, they had no doubt.

Amber Family Trophies

Ava Amber

Albert Amber

Agnes Amber

You're sure
to win.

1st
WINNER - 2016

WINNER - 2012

WINNER - 2008

1st
WINNER - 2004

WINNER - 2000

WINNER - 1996

The **problem** was, poor Alice

(please promise you won't tell)

could not play **ANY** instrument

particularly well.

Too scared to tell her friends the truth

or let her family down,

Alice cried, "What can I do?

How will I win the crown?"

First she tried the **glitzaphone**
but her fingers were too slow,

then she tried the **sparklehorn**
but her "toots" came out too low.

Her **drumming** sounded too offbeat
and the cymbals rang too long!

Rinnnnning

The **glitter chimes**
all clashed together,

CLASH

CLANG

the bells went

ding,

dong,

wrong!

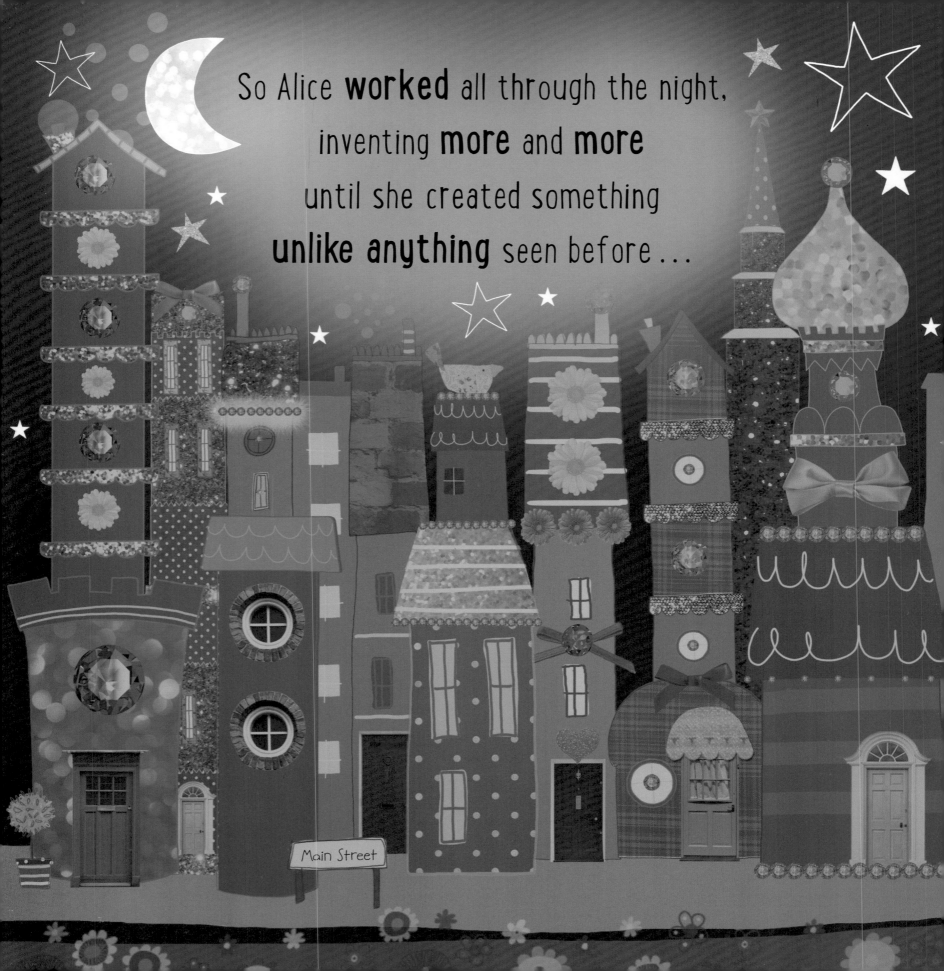

So Alice **worked** all through the night,
inventing **more** and **more**
until she created something
unlike anything seen before...

Main Street

She took a breath, then blew inside
and **without touching a key,**

the instrument played **ON ITS OWN.**

Alice practiced
"**playing**"
to make her
act look true
until she was
finally ready for
her **Showstopper**
debut.

and was **TUNEFUL** as can be!

As Alice watched each one perform
and play their part with pride,
she felt **guilty** about tricking them
and knew she could not lie.

Alice was called to start her piece,
and the crowd let out a cheer
(for Alice's music was the act
they most wanted to hear).

"Umm... before I start," said Alice,
"there's something I **must** say.
I'm not a good musician;
in truth, I **cannot play.**

I **created** this machine
to cover up who I am.
This instrument plays on its own;
I'm really just a **sham**."

The fairies **gasped** together. They hadn't expected that!
As Alice began to tremble, Esme appeared from the back.

Well, that was a surprise.

Oh, my!

She smiled and hugged poor Alice. "Don't feel blue," she said. "You may not be a **Showstopper**, but you're our **inventor** instead."

Alice did not play her piece,
and the **Showstopper** was won
by the most deserving fairy,
chosen by everyone.

Hurrah!

WINNER

Showstopper Spectacular 2017

Well done, Bailey Belle!

Go on, Alice!

WINNER

At the **afterparty** later,
the fairies all agreed:
There was one thing that the party
did really, truly need.

They cried to Alice all at once,
"We want to hear you play!"
So Alice grinned and took a breath
and without further delay . . .

it went...

Toot-Toot, la-de-da,

Though the special instrument
was **famous** near and far,

Alice learned that **best** of all
is being **who you are!**